Praise for Welcome to America

'Knausgård's story of a family in crisis is shocking and imaginative. Everything is written in beautiful and sparse prose which suggests that, after all, from darkness comes light.'
JURY, AUGUST PRIZE

'Knausgård's artistry is masterful.'
Bookslut

'*Welcome to America* presents itself as an étude in the musical sense of the term: a basic theme that varies to infinity, acquiring with each new variation a new unprecedented facet. A triumph.'
Le Monde

'The incandescent *Welcome to America* allows one to discover the author's vibrant and powerful universe.'
Lire

'Gets you in the gut. A delirious dance.'
L'Alsace Quotidien

'A tender novel about a mute girl: gentle, sensitive, minimal, concise, subtle, and brutal. This is writing as self-defense and liberation.'
VOLKER WEIDERMANN. *Spiegel*

D1440427

9580000126213

'A daring and disturbing novel. One will not soon forget the eleven-year-old narrator and her silence.'
MDR Kultur

'In her slim book, Boström Knausgård conjures a constellation reminiscent of a psychological thriller. *Welcome to America* is a book that masterfully describes the many nuances of inner darkness.'
Austria Presse Agentur

'A short, very lyrical novel. The scenes succeed in their great universality, closely observed, wisely questioned.'
Brigitte Woman

'Outstanding psychological chamber play. Linda Boström Knausgård has an incredible ability to give voice to the young narrator's haunting thoughts and she does it through such dense prose that is both simple and powerful, both tangible and poetic.'
Politiken

'Boström Knausgård has her own poetic language. The imagery is just as natural and brilliant as it is mad and askew.'
Dagbladet

LINDA BOSTRÖM KNAUSGÅRD (Sweden) is an author and poet, as well as a producer of documentaries for Swedish radio. Her first novel, *The Helios Disaster*, was awarded the Mare Kandre Prize and shortlisted for the Swedish Radio Novel Award 2014. *Welcome to America*, her second novel, has been awarded the prestigious Swedish August Prize and nominated for the Svenska Dagbladet Literary Prize.

MARTIN AITKEN is a full-time translator of Scandinavian literature. Working mainly from Danish and more recently Norwegian, he has translated the works of writers such as Kim Leine, Helle Helle, Peter Høeg, and Karl Ove Knausgaard. His recent translation of Hanne Ørstavik's *Love* was a finalist for the 2018 National Book Award. *Welcome to America* is his first book from Swedish.

WELCOME TO AMERICA

LINDA BOSTRÖM KNAUSGÅRD

WELCOME TO AMERICA

Translated from the Swedish
by Martin Aitken

WORLD EDITIONS
New York, London, Amsterdam

Published in the USA in 2019 by World Editions LLC, New York
Published in the UK in 2019 by World Editions Ltd., London

World Editions
New York/London/Amsterdam

Printed by Mullervisual/Mart. Spruijt, Amsterdam,
Netherlands

British Library Cataloguing-in-Publication Data
A catalogue record for this book is available on request from
the British Library.

ISBN 978-1-912987-04-7

First published as *Välkommen till Amerika* in Sweden in 2016 by
Modernista. Published by agreement with Copenhagen Literary
Agency ApS, Copenhagen.

The cost of this translation was defrayed by a subsidy from the
Swedish Arts Council, gratefully acknowledged.

Twitter: @WorldEdBooks
Facebook: WorldEditionsInternationalPublishing
www.worldeditions.co.uk

Book Club Discussion Guides are available on our website.

It's a long time already since I stopped talking. They're used to it now. My mum, my brother. My dad's dead, so I don't know what he'd have to say about it. Maybe that it was genetic. The genes come down hard in our family. Hard and without mercy. The direct lines of descendancy. Maybe the silence was always inside me. I used to say things that weren't true. I said the sun was out when it was raining. That the porridge we ate was green like the grass and tasted like soil. I said school was like walking into pitch darkness every day. Like having to hold on to a handrail until it was time to go home. What did I do when school was over? I certainly didn't play with my brother, he locked himself away in his room with his music. He nailed the door shut. He pissed in bottles he kept. It was what they were for.

The silence makes no difference. You

mustn't believe otherwise. You mustn't believe the sun will rise in the morning, because you can't ever be sure it will. I haven't used the notebook my mum gave me. In case there's something you want to communicate, she said. The notebook was a kind of consent. She was accepting my silence. Leaving me alone. At some point it would cease. Most likely it would cease.

I passed my hand over the windowsill and drew outlines in the dust that stuck to my palm. A spruce tree and a Father Christmas. It was all I could think of. Thoughts come so slowly and express themselves so simply: pellets, bread slice, pond.

Did I say we lived in an apartment? There was no contact with nature, apart from the park where I saw my first flasher. I was sitting on top of the climbing frame and the man stood below and exposed himself completely. He took off his pants altogether. His thing was stiff and purple. I stared and noted the colour.

I had friends, but they don't come round anymore. They found other apartments to visit once the silence began. Before that, there were always kids at ours. My mum was bonkers. At ours you could shoot pucks against the double doors. We built a skateboard ramp up against the bookshelves, and the apartment was so big we could roller-skate in it. It made marks in the parquet, but the important thing was for the children to play. The place is quiet now. That's one difference anyway.

I stopped talking when growing began to take up too much space inside me. I was sure I couldn't do both, grow and talk at the same time. I think perhaps I was the sort of person who liked to take charge, and it felt good to give that up. There were so many to keep track of. So many dreams to fulfil. Wish something of me, I could say. But I could never make any wish come true. Not really.

I could have talked about my mum. But I said nothing. I didn't want her glitzy smiles. Her perfect hair. Her wanting me to be a beautiful girl. To her, beauty was something on its own. An important property that had to be cultivated like a flower. You had to sow the seed and make sure to water it so you could watch it grow. I could have been like her. Dark, with a kind of sparkle that went without saying. But somehow I fell short. I was no force of nature, the way she was. I was infected by doubt. It was everywhere. It ran through the marrow of my spine and spread from there. I felt doubt assail me. Days and nights, sunsets awash with doubt.

I wrote nothing in my notebook, but I always knew where it was. I moved it from the top cupboard to under the pillow, then back to the cupboard again. Sometimes I hid it behind the toilet in case I needed to write something there.

My dad's dead. Did I mention that? It's my fault. I prayed out loud to God for him to die and he did. One morning he was lying there motionless in his bed. That was the power there was in me speaking. Maybe what I said about growing wasn't right. Maybe I stopped talking because my wish came true. You think you want your wishes to come true. But you don't. You should never ask for what you want. It disturbs the order of things. The way you really want them.

You want to be disappointed. You want to be hurt and have to struggle to get over it. You want the wrong presents on your birthday. You might think you want what you wish for, but you don't.

The days and nights are the same. The silence softens the edges so everything is like a kind of mist. We can call them half-days. We can call them what we like.

Before, I would often go with my mum to the theatre. I don't do that anymore. I hear her go out and I hear her come back. The last time I saw her perform she was a fallen Statue of Liberty wishing the immigrants welcome to America. She was bald, with a shard of mirror stuck on her brow. She'd lost her torch. I loved it. The way they'd made her up. The way she shone and shone on the stage. Welcome to America. Welcome to America.

I felt an urge to write those exact words in my notebook. But I stopped myself. You've got to be strict. You can't just follow the impulses that criss-cross the mind in their little tunnels of light. I could see my thoughts. They were everywhere. They passed into my body, darting about my heart, toying with it, forcing themselves upon it. I could do nothing about my thoughts.

I sang in the school choir. The music teacher's name was Hildegard. She was from Austria. If only I could sing like you, she wrote in a book I was given as a prize on the last day of term. She did sing dreadfully. Her voice was a screech. But she knew all the parts. I sang on my own that day in the church. *The sun is shining, the grass is green, the orange and palm trees sway, there's never been such a day in Beverly Hills, L.A. But it's December the twenty-fourth, and I am longing to be up north.* I was so nervous I was shaking, but it went down well. And my mum said everyone was always nervous.

My dad spoke to me in a dream. Cat got your tongue? he said. No, daddy. But the words are so heavy. So heavy to fling about.

What more did he say? You're my lovely girl. You were never any trouble. No, daddy, I said. I was never any trouble.

He needed reassuring. Even though he was dead. In that respect, there's no difference between the living and the dead.

I tried to keep him away. Ignored his questions. But he was everywhere, the same as when he was alive. To the fatherland, he'd say, filling up his glass. To the old woman who has no teeth.

It was all so easy. My mum says it was denial. That I wanted life to pass by me, instead of standing there getting drenched in it like everyone else. She thought less of me now, but that was hardly surprising. I thought less of her, too. We were standing on each side of a trench, measuring out a distance between us. Or perhaps we were measuring each other. Measuring each other with our eyes. Who was the stronger? Who was weak? Who would come creeping in the night, sobbing and reaching out to be held?

Nevertheless, she'd been loath to make an issue of it. That's what she told my teacher at school, who after a week was in tears. It's a whim, she said. She's full of them. Don't make a thing about it. Leave her alone. She'll grow out of it again. There's nothing the matter with her.

Along with speech went the light. It no longer danced on the walls where we lived. We're a family of light, my mum would say, though my dad lay in bed staring at the wall when he was alive. What light, my eyes would ask. What light are you talking about? Maybe we'd always measured each other. Maybe the question of who was strong and who was weak had been there from the start.

I was afraid of my brother. Always had been. All the time, he was there, his hands and his rage. My grandma up north sent me a box of raisins. He snatched it from my hand. I lost my temper and picked up a knife. But what was I going to do with a knife? He stood there laughing at me as he filled his face.

I kept a stash in the bathroom, of books, sandwiches, fruit. All hidden away on the top shelf, behind the toilet paper we bought in bulk. As soon as my mum went out and shut the door behind her, my brother would turn on me and I would flee to the bathroom. And there I would sit for hours on end. I read books, or at least tried to make the words stick, but usually the fear meant my eyes just skated about on the page, and I could never remember what they saw. Of course, he would eventually tire of keeping me prisoner, and there was a tacit understanding that at some point he would stop and let me out.

And then we could play together. We played pirates, or pretended we were blind. He only let me play if he could pull my nails out. I closed my eyes and held out my hands. They lay like little windows in his palm when it was done.

Love between siblings. Was that what it was like? He was moody and I was mild. That was how we'd dealt the cards. You can always pass, no matter how good a hand you've got, my dad always said. If you're good enough you can.

I was good. I could be cagey, then lay down a hand of aces when the others were naive enough to fall for it. Card games, pucks flying through the air. The theatre was there always, like a great sky. Was that what I missed the most?

Maybe I just can't get away from my mum

the way I'd like. She's too big, too buoyant, too omnipotent by half. But I try. I see her diamond rings all sticky with dough. I see the strength of her. How wonderful it was to clutch her tight when I was little. Am I grown up now?

I've only just turned eleven. It's fair to say the day was a joke, the birthday song—*Long may she live!*—and the presents tossed at me like I was a dog.

Did I *want* to live? my mum asked me when the cake was eaten. Did I? Her eyes bored into mine.

I'm falling away, were the words that came to me. Words spoken only as thoughts. Repeated over and over again. I'm falling away, I'm falling away from all that is living.

And my sleep at nights. As if I were crossing the sea on stilts. Striding high above the waters, the curve of the earth in front of my eyes.

It could have been worse.

The room is quiet around me. The walls are bare after I pulled down the posters. I sit in the windowsill, looking down at the only tree in the courtyard. A chestnut tree. Music seeps through the wall. My brother's room is next door. Mine is what used to be the maid's room, though spacious like every other in this apartment. The staff here had plenty of room in the old days. There's an entrance from the yard, a secret staircase, a narrow spiral of cast-iron leading to the kitchen. The door is never locked. My mum doesn't care to lock doors. She feels so easily shut in. Sometimes I'm scared I'll talk in my sleep. That someone will hear me and hold it against me at some future time. I see my mum's triumphant face. It wouldn't be right.

The room is dark. But I don't switch on the light. We're a family of light. A light to ourselves. There's a lot that doesn't bear thinking about.

My brother's footsteps as he crosses the floor. The way he moves about in there. Tramping, yet timid at the same time. His voice inside me when he tells me to do something. Take his plate away. Fetch him a glass of water. I'm his servant. Or slave. I do as he says, afraid of his hand, the way it grips my throat. I don't like to think about being afraid of my brother. But I think about it a lot.

Before, there was always the park. I used to play in the tree with my friend. We sat for hours, talking about the world the way we saw it. We were together there in the tree, and we climbed higher and higher, until at last we sat at the very top, each in our own fork, with legs that dangled down. Now she plays with another girl. I don't know if they climb the tree. But I saw them skipping across the school playground, the way we always did, where one abruptly bolts like a horse, pulling the other along with her. The panic that struck between her strides, converting into sudden acceleration. Their laughter, which sounded like crying.

The smell of my mum. Her perspiration in sleep. The warm bulk of her body to snuggle up to and sleep beside. Her heavy breathing, in and out. The bedroom, with its velvet curtains and the picture on the wall. The framed diploma from the academy of dramatic arts above the table and telephone. The black garter draped over the picture, a souvenir from some show or other. The ashtray of brown glass. My mum's room, smelling always of stale smoke and naked body. Or exhaust fumes when she opened the window in the mornings to let in the air. The street separated the building and the park. The cars drove fast. They took chances, accelerating to catch the lights before they changed. We lived splendidly, overlooking the park. Six rooms and a kitchen. My mum needed a fair amount of income. She took pupils in the living room. When I came home from school I would hear her smooth voice and the efforts of her pupils in there. The dramas of the world echoed around the apartment. We got used to it. Our friends did too, though we always had to explain the situation to begin with. The screams and the laughter. We were supposed to be quiet when mum had her pupils, or else play outside. When her classes were over, she would open the doors of the living room wide, as if to show us we were allowed to enter. The walls seemed still to tremble with the nerves of her pupils. But after a few laps on our roller skates, through the bathroom, into the great drawing room with the door that led out onto the balcony, into the serving corridor with its black-and-white chequered flooring, and back into the living room again, it was as if the room once more was ours. We practised our starts in the hall. From zero to a hundred, the front door was our brake. My brother had his friends. I had mine. It was mostly his who practised their ice-hockey shots against the door, leaving it peppered with black marks, but sometimes we joined in, me and my friends, dribbling forward and sending the puck skidding across the floor. Sometimes I went to my friends' houses as well, but the smells there, and the sense of order I always found, confused me. I would long to go home. I would long for my mum. Her hands, her solicitude. I would long to be biking along the pavement with her, on our way home from the theatre in the dark light of evening. Always on the pavement, even if it was against the law. People would shame us as we came whooshing along, invariably at top speed, as if the speed were vital to us in some way, as if it kept us alive. My mum talked us out of trouble the time we got stopped by the police. It was easy for her.

But when she cried, the world fell apart and her crying was all there was. The guttural sounds she made, and all that came out of her. It was like setting a match to me, hearing her cry. Sometimes she could be on the phone at the same time. All this responsibility, she could wail, and it was as if my whole being zeroed in on her weeping so that I might understand and make it better. I took her distress in my hands as if it were a tangle of threads, and tried to unravel them, one at a time, to stop her tears by being there to help, but sometimes there was nothing I could do, the tears would be that much stronger.

I hear my brother on the other side of the wall. He's built his own sound studio in there. Mixer board, speakers, cables. Sometimes he'll bring some nice-looking girl home with him after school for her to sing his songs. He empties his bottles of piss in the night when no one can see, and hides them away if anyone comes to visit. Maybe he puts them under the bed. My brother can do what he wants. No one's ever been bothered. Maybe I could too. The thing is my own will is too weak to surface. If I had to probe into my life and ask myself questions, I wouldn't be able to answer.

On weekdays I walk to school. To begin with I wore pleated skirts and a woolen Loden coat, pigtails flapping against my back. No one else dressed like that, but I didn't realise. Now I wear jeans and a top like everyone else. The school smells of dust and chalk and damp clothing. Always the same smell, though the spring draws in more dust and the dampness can recede. I never write on the board or in my books. Not speaking and not writing are the same. I can't do one thing and not the other. Our teacher's name is Britta. She speaks to my mum on the phone once a week. They talk about me, and I'm not sure if I like that or not. The days pass quickly. I walk to school and then I'm walking home again. What happens in between is something I absorb. I feel the way the class seems to proceed through the days like a living organism; suddenly someone will break out and pull others with them, but their agitation diminishes, everything evens out and becomes stable again. I listen carefully to what the teacher has to say, and I put her words away inside me. In the dining hall I keep to myself, sit on my own and eat my lunch. No one speaks to me anymore, and the memory of myself at school, the games we played, the way I took charge, has begun to fade.

The walk home. Seeing the entranceway of our building always gives me a kind of shock. The marble columns and statues, a man and a woman holding up the balcony of the apartment above ours, the only one facing the street. The paintings on the stairway, the angels on the ceiling, the stone stairs with the fossils in them. We live on the first floor. The key slides into the lock, the door opening into the hall with the piano I sometimes played without being able. Home, home. Before, there was my dad to consider, the mood he might be in and what he could do. You never knew if it was going to be a quiet afternoon or if he'd be wanting company. But I didn't need to worry about that anymore. Death stood between us now, like a river running by, and I could wade through that river, across to the other shore, and know I was safe.

My mum's thick, blond hair, her wide mouth and full lips, her laughter, so vibrant and fluid. So much joy. In one seamless movement, upwards, ever upwards, she could lift me and I would rise with her, rise to the ceiling and out into space, we rose and rose together. We flew. Flew over the city, looking down at the rooftops below, laughing as we picked out our own, onwards, upwards, away into the world. The air grew thin and cold, darkness surrounded us, until we turned and fell through the layers, all the way back to the apartment, and were again standing in our living room with the view of the park. It was night and thundering. Lightning lit up the park, the trees showed themselves fleetingly to us as light, before darkness took over again. Mum laughed at my fear of thunder. I had come running to her, crying, and we stood there together in the middle of the floor, staring into the night as it was ripped apart by electricity, and she laughed. What more did she do? Did she go with me back to my room again? Did she sit with me, on the edge of the bed? I can't remember.

Maybe this was where I should have resisted. Resisted the memories. I sat here in the darkness thinking about her, even though I didn't want to. What did I want?

I wanted to sit in enduring silence, to feel it grow strong and take everything into its possession. Was that what I wanted? Yes, that too.

I surveyed the room. The bunk beds with the curtain mum had sewn, the night table with the books I no longer read, left there. The desk and the floral armchair where my clothes were dumped, the ones that weren't in the wardrobe. The flowery wallpaper. Why were there so many flowers in my room?

I went to the kitchen, knowing no one was there. I filled a glass with water and scurried back, drank the water and put the glass down on the desk. The notebook lay there with its soft, black cover. I ran my hand across it. Something inside me liked it being there.

The first time I went to see my dad at the hospital he showed me off to everyone: patients, nurses, doctors. He was jaunty, glowing almost as he told them: This is my daughter. This is my daughter. He couldn't sit still, he went off into the day room where the TV and the games were. I made sure not to look anyone in the eye. Mostly, I stared at the floor. A doctor sent him back to his room. Sit here and stay with your daughter, he said, and closed the door when he went out. It was as if suddenly dad came down to earth. He said: I'm no good. I'm no good. Several times in a row. He looked down at his hands, I at mine, until the visit was over and I could leave the ward and go back to mum who was waiting in the cafeteria.

That was the first time. There were some more visits after that. And then mum no longer wanted him to live with us, so he went and lived on his own in a flat. I never felt guilty about wishing he was dead. It was the best thing.

Sometimes, though, I felt guilty about him being on his own. At home he'd had us, even when all he could do was lie on the sofa, though occasionally, if he was up to it, he might make dinner after we'd played cards.

We were a family of light. Mum's light shone out to us all. Her light poured on us. Before, I'd been proud of my mum. The most beautiful of all the mothers at the parents' evening. Conversing with the teacher and the other parents. She made an impression. No one could resist her. Least of all me. And could I now? Resist her? Was my silence down to her? How could anyone allow someone else to take up so much space in their lives?

You're only a child, she used to say, lifting my chin to make me look at her. You're only a child, and now it's enough. Do you hear me? Enough.

I saw my brother in the playground. I saw him, and he saw me.

The first few days had been a rush of excitement. The fact that I could. That it was so easy. Just stopping. From one moment to the next my life was changed. It was more than a refusal.

It wasn't running away. It was the truth. The truth about me.

Now and then I wondered what my voice would sound like if all of a sudden one day I said something. Whether it was still there inside me, waiting, or if it was gone. What would it sound like? That was one question I asked myself.

I asked myself others too, like about responsibility. Was I making my mum go mad? Most often she was calm, but when she flipped it felt as if it was my fault. It wasn't so much what she said, it was more that she became small all of a sudden. I made her small. It was scary. I wondered whether I had to start talking again to stop her from disappearing. If I had to choose between her and myself, wouldn't I choose her?

Wouldn't I choose her strength over mine?

Yes. I would. That was still the way it was.

Sleep came like a mist in the night. It settled over me, only a few centimetres of air between me and it. I filled that air with a prayer. Always the same: *Dear God who art in Heaven. Look after mum. Make her happy and never let anything bad happen to her. Amen.*

Make her happy. God makes her happier than I can. Every night I prayed for her, and how I knew God was listening I've no idea. I just knew. I had access to God. It was me and God who'd killed my dad. We'd done it together, once and for all. God and me.

At night, I went about the apartment making sure everything was the way it was supposed to be. That things were in their proper places in the kitchen. That the balcony door was shut. I stood for a long time in the living room looking at the moonlight over the park. I put the chain on the front door, went to my mum's bedroom and listened to her deep breathing. It was unthinkable for me now to climb in beside her, the way I did when I was little. The thought repelled me, but I still liked to look at her when she was asleep. For some reason it made me feel good to know that she was at rest. That she would be at rest until morning, when she would get up and sprinkle bilberries over our yoghurt, take the grapefruit juice that all of us liked so much from the fridge and pour it into our glasses, butter the bread for us, despite our being old enough to do it ourselves. She wanted to be present in the mornings, to be there for us. That was what she said: I want to be there for you. That was probably the worst thing: that I wouldn't let her be there for me. That I wouldn't accept anything of what she was giving.

I was always quiet before, at the theatre too. Mum was annoyed by it, but there was so much for her to do that it got lost in everything else. At performances, I was allowed to sit next to the prompter, and there my silence was expected. It would have been terrible if I'd suddenly started talking in the theatre space. Unthinkable. But after, in the corridors and walkways to and from the dressing room or the rehearsal rooms, whenever mum spoke to me she would surely have appreciated an answer, but it was like it was impossible for me to speak in that building. That the only thing I could do was look at my mum, look at her over and over again. Follow her transformations from beginning to end.

Silence had always been there as a possibility. A black floor to step out on.

Have I mentioned our getaway cabin? It burned down. To begin with we were there in the summer and at weekends. Cooped up inside its brown-painted walls. In the evenings we put the nets out, mum, dad, my brother, and me. I would sit in the prow and look out over the water that glittered in the mornings, and loomed up at me, slate blue, in the evenings. My brother scooped up the trapped fish, hauling them up into the boat with the landing net. We filled our crates with slippery fish—whitefish, cod, the occasional turbot—and afterwards mum would prepare them, fish pudding with melted butter. It was at the cabin dad started to change. One night he stopped us sleeping by singing the compère's song from *Cabaret* for hours on end. There were noughts-and-crosses tournaments. He drank all the time.

Eventually, mum phoned the hospital and an ambulance came and took him away. The first time he was locked up, I felt a stillness spread through my body, like warmth. He was gone. For the time being he was gone, and I hadn't realised it was what I'd been wanting all along, for him not to be there.

I saw photographs of the cabin on fire. A boy on the road had taken pictures with his camera. I saw the flames, the way the blaze took hold of the structure with all its might, consuming it. Later, my brother and I picked through the ashes and the question we asked ourselves hung unuttered in the air between us: Was it dad? Was it dad who started the fire?

There were a lot of questions like that, hanging unuttered between my brother and me.

My brother took dad's death as if it were the most natural thing in the world. It was he who'd answered when the nurse phoned from the hospital. She asked for mum, but mum wasn't in. You can tell me, my brother said. Is it dad? He must have sounded older on the phone than he was, because the nurse told him everything. Dad had been lying there for three weeks, no one had asked about him. It was the nurse who'd found him. He hadn't turned up to his last few appointments and, because he wasn't answering the phone either, a doctor had asked the nurse to go to his flat and check up.

He was dead. All at once, great spaces opened inside me. Spaces the silence filled. An immense calm came over me in the beginning, and the sense that this was what had always been missing.

I never let on to anyone about me, God, and my dad. That knowledge was something I had to bear myself.

What else did my thoughts say? They lurked and pounced on me. They were noisy, and I batted the air with my hands, the way you do to swat a fly. I chased my thoughts away. I didn't want them, but the thoughts were big and strong. They knew I was only a child. That there was nothing I could do to stand up to them. I imagined a whole life with such thoughts and realised it would be impossible. Peering ahead in time is dangerous. You never know what you might see. I needed to stay where I was.

There was a question I asked myself: What did it mean to be grown up? How did you know when you were?

Dad had been out in the boat when the fire started in the cabin. By the time he got back it was ablaze. What thoughts were going through him, watching his dream go up in flames? He loved fishing. We went on trips to the nearby islands. The picnic basket was always full. Mum made sure of everything: squash, sandwiches, coffee, biscuits. We explored the island, and after that we fished. I learned to use the oars when the outboard ran out of petrol one day. My brother and I sat with an oar each and chopped through the water together. We had been together. All of us. And now we weren't. Had I always been scared of my dad? Yes, always.

I often pictured him dead. I imagined the moment he died. How his heart stopped beating from one second to the next. His final breath. I imagined he was happy, but the thought was tainted. How long had he been in the flat? How long since he spoke to someone? It was the loneliness that came across the strongest when I pictured him in front of me.

I wanted to draw him dead, but I couldn't. I wanted to draw the fine lines of his face. His staring eyes.

Once, I forgot the key. I'd been needing a wee for ages at school, and hurried home as fast as I could. I stood there at the front door, ringing the bell in desperation, but by the time my brother answered I'd already wet myself. There was a puddle at my feet on the landing, and me standing there crying. My brother got me changed and put me to bed. As if I was ill. Then he cleaned up the mess on the landing.

*

Darkness was everywhere. The darkness smelled. It smelled of fright and something sickly. Darkness it was that rushed from the tap and filled up the bath. I washed my hair in darkness, my body, my entire being. I ate of the darkness, and was stained by it inside. The darkness encroached. Only mum still contained the light. Darkness yielded to her. Unburdened, she went about as if it were nothing. Even if her brow was now furrowed. We're a family of light, were the words that came out, with the same conviction as ever. I wondered if she even saw the darkness. If it frightened her. If she was refusing to see it, or if it really wasn't there for her.

I kept a knife in the drawer of my desk. I sometimes took it out and looked at it. Felt the sharpness of the blade against my fingertips. It was the filleting knife that we used to bone fish, and how it ever came to be in the hall one day, so conspicuous there on the window sill, I've no idea. But I took it with me into my room and put it in the drawer, and its being there gave me a feeling of calm. I had a knife. Now and then I took it out of the drawer and placed it on top of the notebook, where it was plain to see how sharp it was. I wondered if I would ever use it.

The bass thumped in my brother's room,

throbbing at the wall. Maybe he was laying a bass track down on the computer. It was the only instrument I could hear. My brother's musical talents had held my mum's attention from the start. She bought him whatever he pointed at in the music store, which was quite a lot. He played the guitar and the piano. I'd never heard him practise. All of a sudden he could just play.

Before, I would sing to his music, into the microphone, and he would mix the song and we would listen to it all together, mum, my brother, and me. Mum always said the same thing: that my brother was brilliant and I sang so well. That we were musical was something she took to be a good sign. It fit in with us being a family of light. It had been a long time now since my brother had wanted to share anything with us. He kept mum firmly from his room by nailing it shut, and I wouldn't ever have dreamed of knocking on his door. The three of us kept to ourselves. Mum was at the theatre, I didn't even know what she was playing. By the time she got home late in the evenings I was usually asleep, or else I would hear her and not get up. All this must have been a hindrance to her in her efforts to look on the bright side. The silence around me grew and became their silence too. Mum still spoke to me, but she stopped expecting me to answer. I think I'd have given her a fright if I'd suddenly said something. It feels as if every situation strives to find balance, each encounter at the fridge, that every moment is something that has to be poised against something else. Living together was perhaps just that, shifting the centre of balance until everyone could stick it out. There were lots of ways. One was no better than the rest.

They're growing up, mum would say to a girlfriend over the phone. Soon they won't be children anymore. But it was only something she said. That wasn't what was happening at all. Not yet.

What *was* happening? Were we coming apart now that dad had gone? Had he been keeping us together? Why did I no longer belong in my family?

Dear God. Look after mum and make her happy. Amen. Her happiness was the most important of all. I could have done a lot more. I could have talked to her. I could have been like I was in school. I could have filled the apartment with voices and life. Did it ever occur to me what life would be like without her? What we would do then on our own? It was a thought that didn't bear thinking. She was everything to me. Without her I couldn't exist. I knew that.

I used to have a life. Did I still? My refusal to speak was bigger than I had ever been. The silence came out of me and laid itself over everything that was here. It went into mum's mouth and reshaped her words. Absorbed her syllables. Are you hungry? Have you showered today? Have you done your homework?

Before, the words would tumble out in her eagerness to describe the world. To express her joy at being alive.

How did she end up in the theatre? Mum and dad lived together up north, she was a secretary at the iron works, he was an engineer. He had his fishing and his football, a job he enjoyed, and then she came and messed it up. How small a life, she would say. Is this all there is? She took the train down south, to the capital, applied to the country's finest drama school and was admitted. It was sheer grit. Her new class were on the TV news, and dad and grandma and everyone else up there saw her sitting on the stone steps of the Royal Dramatic Theatre, waving at the camera with all the others. They relocated and she began her new life. Dad had to end his and tag along. It was the start of his decline. He couldn't hack it in the city, even though he soon got a new job and supported mum during the years she attended the school.

I used to tell her everything. She could get me to talk about the slightest fluctuation. It was such a blessing, the way she always knew how I felt, and together we could thrash things out, bring them into the open, until the badness was little and all on its own, and vanished in the light, her light. She took all the badness and made it go away. She was a magician, playing with the light on the walls, stealing into the nooks and crannies of my mind, slipping into my tummy, where the badness first set in. She soothed me from the inside and made me free. When had it stopped? How could I have chosen to be without it? To be without her?

Was that the difference between the child and the grown-up? To be able to let light in, and then not? What was I now? I wasn't a grown-up. But I wasn't a child either. I wasn't yet a teenager, so I was a child. A child clinging to darkness. It was scary.

The walls moved in the night. Bulging in and out. As if they were breathing. I put my hands against them, pressed to keep them still, but they kept on breathing and took no notice. Sometimes I sat on the balcony in the night and looked at the stars. Looked for the constellations I knew. There weren't many: the Plough, the Little Bear, the Great Bear. When I was little we used to drag the mattresses and covers out to the balcony in summer and sleep there. One night, dad came shinning up the drainpipe. He was tired of his flat, but mum had taken his key to ours. His eyes flashed in the darkness as he climbed onto the balcony and we looked at each other. He could turn up anytime. He always turned up. His dark eyes that night. The look that silenced me straight away. The look that said he was going to kill us.

One time we came home from visiting grandma up north, the whole apartment was filled with gas. Dad had turned it on and the air was thick and hard to breathe. Mum ran down into the street with me and my brother and told us to wait on the pavement. Then she dashed back up into the apartment, turned off the gas, and opened the windows. My brother there in the street with my hand in his: You know mummy can die, don't you? But then she came back down and we went to a café where we stuffed ourselves to celebrate that we were still alive. Later, when evening came, I heard her talking to dad on the phone. Were you trying to kill us?

The nights were crisp and clear on the balcony. We had two big wicker chairs out there with cushions, and a small table with a lantern on it. Mum often smoked a cigarette on the balcony after dinner and I would watch her from the kitchen while I did the dishes. All I could see was the smoke curling into the air, the back of her head, her blond hair. Perhaps she sat with her feet up on the rail. Perhaps she was trying to relax and remove herself from it all. My mum's solitude was something I couldn't think about.

The terror I felt if she didn't come straight home after the show. My crying if it got too late. Where was she? What had happened? Most likely she was only having a drink with the others. She was seldom late, but when she was that was what I told myself she was doing.

The clock, sweeping away the time, and her not being back. I used to lie down on the sofa in the living room and wait. I waited and waited. Now I did the same, but in my bed, and the tears would never come. The relief of hearing her key in the door was still the same though. She had survived. She was alive.

Before, the thought never occurred to me that she probably needed to see other people besides my brother and me. The thought was new to me and it came out of the silence along with every other understanding. She wanted to be with other grown-ups. Nothing odd about that.

Sometimes I would think I was punishing her. That I was attacking all the light with my darkness.

I ate my dinners in my room. Fetched my plate from the kitchen, with meat and rice, chicken or fish. Always something well prepared, from fresh ingredients. I couldn't refuse food. My hunger was too great and I imagined myself to be growing with every bite I took. That I was nourishing my growth and that it was no use stopping. I was nearly the tallest in my class by then. From having been one of the smallest I'd now shot up. There was something uncomfortable about growing like that, it felt so out of control. I even pestered God about it, pleading with him to stop me growing so fast. I knew I could make it stop by speaking. As things were, there was nothing to curb it, nothing in its way.

My mum would leave a tray at my brother's door. When no one was there, he opened the door and took it in. Then he would nail the door shut again and eat. There was no need for the nails. Neither mum nor I would ever go in there.

But sometimes mum came into my room. She could stand for a long time in the middle of the floor, looking around. As if barely awake, unable to take things in. Her gaze passed over me and warmed me in the armchair. If I was sitting on the bed she would sometimes sit down beside me and smooth my hair. Everything all right? she might say, and look at me, only in the next instant to vanish inside herself. Getting enough fresh air? Why don't you go over to the park for a bit? I wouldn't move, but did my utmost not to shake or nod my head. Please yourself, she would say and then leave. The room had to catch up with itself again after her visits. It needed to settle down and get its breath back. I put my hand against the wall and pressed against it to see if it would give, but it stayed the way it was, motionless. She left her smell behind her when she went. The sweet bodily aroma that was hers. I opened the window to the chestnut tree and the evening sky. I sat on the windowsill and looked out over the rear courtyard, the little lawn there under the tree, the gravel pathways that led around the courtyard and from the iron gate to the door. The concierge's old Volvo under its tarps, driven only on the occasional evening in summer.

Now and again they spoke to each other. My mum and my brother. They could laugh together, and I would try not to listen. They seemed to have a kind of shared understanding then. But it was on my brother's terms. Sometimes he needed to come out from his room. Sometimes he needed to talk to mum. About music, school, girls. He'd met someone and wanted to bring her home so mum could meet her too. He was proud of her; it showed. Would she change anything? I asked myself. Would she change my brother? Curb his anger, extinguish it? I looked forward to her coming. I wanted to see her and my mum together.

My brother stopped nailing his door shut. The day before she was meant to come, he left it open. I heard him vacuuming and getting rid of all the bottles. He'd decided to step out into the world. He was done with something, whatever it was.

Mum wanted her to stay for dinner. It was her night off and she asked my brother what they would like to eat. Nothing out of the ordinary, was all he said, but I could hear the way he smiled when he said it. The apartment had life again. Not just mum's pupils, but a proper guest. The kitchen was a hive of expectation, mum busied herself making a seafood pie. Seafood pie, would that be all right?

It was as if my brother had given her a present. At last, a break in our daily lives. I thought it best to keep a distance, so my brother wouldn't need to introduce his sister. No need to bring anything weird into it from the start. Nevertheless, I'd be disconcertingly close to them if they sat in the kitchen, and I thought maybe mum would realise this and set the table in the living room.

All of a sudden, she was there. Her presence could be felt throughout the apartment. The air was different, and I could sense that she too was a person of light. That my brother had found a girlfriend who in many ways was like mum. Her voice, rising and falling with mum's and my brother's. But still it was odd, I thought. That he'd brought her here.

They ate in the living room. Mum had already set the table. I couldn't hear anything of what they said to each other. I listened, but heard only a faint murmur from behind the door. Did I want to be with them? No, not at all. Maybe she would come back. Sooner or later, we would have to be introduced. Perhaps I would hold her hand.

I was sitting in the kitchen when mum came in to put the coffee on. I could tell she was still pleased. Do you want to join us for dessert? Her voice caught me off guard, though I'd seen her come in. I went to my room. To my surprise, she came after me. Her name's Vendela, she said. Perhaps you know her? But I didn't. It had been a long time since I'd looked in the school yearbook and studied the faces of those in the older classes. Maybe you should come out and say hello? Mum put her arm in mine and nudged me gently in the direction of the serving passage. I offered no resistance, allowing myself to be led across the floor to the living room. I saw them sitting at the table, my brother and this Vendela. They looked up at me, and I stepped towards her on my own. She stood up and seemed to collect herself, her features came together. She put her hand out and I shook it. Neither of us said anything. Unexpectedly, my brother got to his feet and said: Vendela, this is my sister who doesn't speak. Vendela smiled at me. I couldn't smile back.

I finished my ice cream and stared down at my plate. Mum chatted with Vendela and my brother. About school mostly, and Vendela's voice rose and fell as various subjects cropped up. Mum was beaming. Energetic and warm. My brother was surprisingly buoyant. Our eyes met over the ice cream and he was wide open. I'd never see him like that before, and sucked in my breath, sensing that something I knew had now come to an end. That something new had begun and that I didn't know what it was. Fiercely, I longed for the way things had been before Vendela. Each of us in our own silence. Now everything was a turmoil. It was opening up and I didn't want that. I would need to get even better at shutting myself in if this was how it was going to be. I got up from the table and crossed the floor. Behind me they went on with their conversation. It was as if I didn't exist. They'd made up their minds, my mum and my brother. I wasn't going to spoil anything.

The walls bulged in my room. I didn't bother pressing my hand against them, but threw myself on the bed and buried my head under the pillow. Nevertheless, I could still hear my brother and Vendela when they went into my brother's room. I heard their voices, my brother putting music on. Vendela's voice sang out into the room. Had they been recording while I'd been at school? It sounded gorgeous, the music and her voice, which seemed almost to float on its own. They laughed in unison about something, and I wondered if my brother was glad she was there or if he'd rather everything were the same as before. Maybe both, I thought to myself, and pulled the cover up.

When I woke up it was night. I sat up with the feeling I'd missed something important. Under what circumstances had she left? Assuming she'd actually gone? Or was she asleep beside my brother in his bed? I went out into the kitchen and through the serving passage, past the living room into the hall. Her shoes weren't there. She must have gone.

I went back to my room. Night was the time I liked best. The silence, and the feeling of everything having wound down to collect itself again before morning. The darkness in which to rest. Nothing that had to be done, or not be done. Stillness. Mum and my brother asleep. I could sit in the armchair and do nothing. What had their parting been like? Had he kissed her while we were here, so close in the apartment? Or had he simply hugged her and breathed in the smell of her hair?

Night was a friend. Silence wasn't odd at night, and loneliness unfeigned. Not like in the daytime, where my silence was more a reaction against mum or my brother. I was one with the night and we spoke the same language. Breathed the same stillness. It was like when I was little and would sit on mum's knee after a performance. The way I could sleep there in her lap and not have to be afraid of anything. Just give up and sail away. The way mum would lay me down on the sofa in the dressing room while she got changed. Removed her makeup, moisturised, pulled off the wig cap with all the hair pins she kept in a glass jar. All of this I sensed in sleep, the way you sense something happen above the surface while swimming deep underwater. You see a movement, but are far away, the water pressing against your ear drums. The last cigarette before she would wake me up and we'd go down into the foyer and ask them to call a taxi. I sleep-walked into the lift, descended six floors, before lying down again with my head in mum's lap in the back of the cab. Absorbing her fragrance and the leathery smell of the upholstery. The lights in the night as we drove. The street lamps suspended like small, shining planets. The cab door after we got out and it was shut behind us. The cold air as we crossed the pavement to the entranceway. The stairs up to the apartment, and mum putting me to bed with my clothes still on. I was awake and not awake. Like now.

Daddy. Are you there? Yes, I'm here. What do you think of Vendela? Don't worry yourself about her. Mind your own. Do you think I should start talking again? Mum wants me to see a specialist. You'll be fine, petal. You're stronger than them. Am I? Yes, much.

The night wrapped me up inside it, drew me back to bed with its darkness. I listened to the sound of my breathing as it slowed, then drifted into sleep, wading into the water, my dress held up above my knees, crossing over to the island where we bathed when we were away at the cabin. The island where mum had discovered you were allowed to be naked. Only women and children bathed there. The water, salt and sweet, cold and warm against my bare skin. How I swam, back and forth between the island and the jetty. Back and forth. My body finding purchase in every stroke to forge ahead. The sun shone always. The frozen meatballs thawed on the rocks and the sandwiches with liver paste and cucumber in their little packages of silver foil at the bottom of the cooler box would be squashed flat, but always they tasted so good. The bottle of squash, the liquid inside tasting of strawberries and warm plastic. The nudity was confusing. Mum's body, and the cabin neighbours'. Their bare skin. And my own nakedness. I covered myself with the towel when I came up from the water. Mum laughed. What a shy girl. Everyone thought it was funny. Everyone laughed, whatever my mum said. They admired her. It was hard not to.

I hadn't the courage to stare at the naked bodies and would look away, into the water. Dad was up at the cabin seeing to his nets. He shook them apart where they were tangled and hung them up between two nails. He mended the holes. He'd filleted the fish, and the discarded offal lay baking in the sun.

That was how I liked to think about my dad. At the boat, fishing. He was good at that. Everything else was a mess. It was frightening. His eyes in the dark when he shinned up the drainpipe. Or the times we were at grandma's. All of a sudden he could turn up and sit down at the kitchen table, the rage pulsing inside him. Or maybe it was despair. We couldn't keep him away. Just you try, his eyes would say, passing from one of us to the other. My mum could come apart then, disintegrate. The efforts she made to keep him at bay, and then there he was. Sometimes they let him out from the hospital without telephoning first. Well before he was recovered. It was hard to keep someone in against their will. There were special criteria to be met. The knot in my stomach grew into a thumping fist whenever I saw him. Whenever he saw me. He saw that we were afraid and it made him furious. There was nothing wrong with him, how could there be? It was mum there was something wrong with. She was hysterical and wanted him locked up. Flustered, grandma would serve boiled coffee and homemade buns, back and forwards with the coffee pot between the stove and the table: Is that Stig come now? Go on, dip in. A person has to be able to get divorced, mum would say to dad later on. There's no point in anything else if one party doesn't want to go on. You can't just barge in and claim everything back. That was what he wanted. To get us back. He couldn't come to terms with the divorce. It didn't exist for him. We couldn't live without him. But we could. And much better too. Was it at grandma's up north that I first prayed to God?

I thought of killing him myself. I wondered how I could get my hands on my uncle's hunting rifle. I fantasised about thrusting the knife into his chest and twisting it around. It wasn't something I wanted to do, but it was so vital he went away I reasoned that extraordinary measures were called for. I was a child, I wouldn't go to prison. What would happen to me if I killed my dad? Would I be put into care? I didn't know, and so I decided on prayer. His death was in reach. That was how it felt. He was moving about in its presence, of his own accord. The fire. The drainpipe. He climbed up on the roof when he was drunk and often got into fights. Or maybe he would do the deed himself when the pendulum swung the other way and he became mute and consumed by self-loathing. He could hang himself or throw himself off his balcony. All I needed was some time and God, who would help me. *Dear God. Please make my father die. I want him to die and you have to help me. Let's do it now. Together. You and I. Let's kill him. It's my highest wish. Amen.*

Every night the same prayer. Every day and night on earth. The same words. The same wish. Until the night he really did die, in his sleep. He reached for me that night. He came to me as a light in my dream and held out his hand. I think of it as his dying moment. That it was me he was reaching for. Did he know that it was me who killed him? Whether he did or not, he reached for me.

It was as if we all breathed out after his death, though in different ways. Mum was relieved, if somewhat concerned about our now being fatherless. It was worst for my brother. Some of his memories were fond, he kept hold of them and couldn't let go. Perhaps he felt guilty about feeling relieved? For me it was painless. From the moment my brother stood there with the phone in his hand and said that dad was dead, I have been calm.

Is that true? Part of me, at least, has been calm. The part that had to do with him. There was no better ending than the one that came. The solitude, then? The three weeks he lay there? Yes, that was right too.

Sometimes I wonder if I'm bad. If there's something wrong with me. My ability to empathise. Is there something lacking in me? Something important?

Dad's death was a triumph for me and God. It was our first collaboration.

Did I believe in God? Yes, I believed. With all my strength, I believed in God. There was nothing else.

Were we actually a family of darkness? Tormented by secrets and turmoil? But there was mum and her character. The force of nature she was. Withstanding everything.

I used to say that Heaven was like the trees. That the earth contained tunnels all the way down to Hell. That the Devil himself sat listening to what the children said to each other. I said he counted them as his own from when they were small. I said that eternal damnation was the life we were living then, repeated into infinity. And then there were the little lies: I said I was the riding instructor's assistant and that I had three horses of my own, that I kept a silver shark in the bath at home. What I thought I could achieve by such lies I have no idea, but they popped out of me whenever I opened my mouth at school. They couldn't be helped. I was powerless against them, and they were so small. I was so much bigger than them. Now I was living the truth. Not even my thoughts were tainted by lies. Or was I really still lying about something? Something I couldn't see?

It was night and my brother was in love. Mum had surely slept soundly after Vendela's visit. Everything had gone so well. Only I yearned for before. What was it exactly I yearned for? The hallowedness. The silence. What else? Whenever the thought came to me that one day I might speak again, I knotted up inside. What could be worth saying out loud? What could be so important? Mention of the specialist came as a surprise. Mum wasn't letting me be after all. It wasn't going to pass over on its own. It needed a specialist. Had he or she already been contacted? Was there an appointment mum was keeping secret? Was she going to surprise me one day and just take me there? What was expected of me at the consultation? What would the waiting room look like? I immediately imagined a space not unlike that at Odvik the dentist's, with mirrors and magazines, nicely done out in the hallway of an apartment on the square where mum bought flowers and fruit. What would the specialist say? And then the important question: Would mum be in the consulting room with me, or would we be on our own? How would he or she address me, refer to me?

I imagined the way the situation could pan out. The specialist pressing and prodding my body, as if to find an answer there. The chatty way he or she would talk to me, as if I were a much smaller child. How had it started, this refusal to speak? Did I ever forget and say something by mistake? Had anything happened to bring it on? I needed to observe the specialist, try to understand the person he or she was, where their thoughts were and what was behind them. Will. The will of the specialist against my own, who would be strongest? Forever the same question when it came to human beings. Whose will was strongest? What would I have to do to obey my will?

There were too many questions and too few answers. Nevertheless, the fact of the matter was that no one could force me. Not mum, and certainly not some specialist. There were no two ways about it. My refusing to speak was stronger and far more unambiguous than all their attempts to break it down. Only now had I become unambiguous to myself. Everything I had said and done before seemed unnatural, as if I had removed myself further and further from the person I was every time I spoke. It was so much better now. Vendela. Did she really scare me? Was I bothered by her being at home with us? Would it matter if the apartment was full of my brother's friends all absorbed in each other? No. It wouldn't matter at all. Not really. I'd have to withdraw even further. That was all.

I found some photos of her one day. They were lying in a pile face-up on the kitchen table. I could only imagine that my brother wanted us to see them. He would hardly have put them there otherwise. She was naked in them. In one, her whole face was a smile, she was lying on my brother's bed with her legs wide apart. In another she was on all fours. Her bottom took up the whole frame. It was impossible to stop looking at them, and it was obvious my brother had taken them himself. I stared at her mouth, her nakedness, it felt like I was burning inside. It had to do with life itself. Deep down, I knew that. That it was life, burning inside me.

Mum's men. Men who came late at night and left early in the morning. Did it bother me? Or when she threw a party for the last night of a run and the whole ensemble came piling in? Life, going on with me at its edge. Did it bother me that I wasn't in its midst like everyone else? That I was an onlooker? Did I not yearn to plunge myself headlong into life like all the rest? Had I not become complacent, observing from the wings? Was it not cowardly of me? They were living, connecting with each other. They had pluck, whereas I was a despicable coward.

I woke up to find my mum standing in my room. She wanted sleeping bags from the wardrobe, she said. She sleepwalked a lot. I nearly blurted out: The sleeping bags aren't in there, we're not going on any trip, you can go back to bed. It was a close call, so close it made my heart thud in my chest, the thought of those almost uttered words. She rummaged about in the wardrobe and I sat up straight and watched her, breathing quickly in and out, trembling. The words had been there on my lips, ready to be spoken. All I had to do was open my mouth and they'd have come out. I asked my heart to stop beating so hard. I tried to calm myself with the thought that nothing had happened. It had been an impulse, that was all. But somehow mum's sleepwalking had forced me out of my shell. Suddenly I'd wanted to reach out to her with my voice. Only it hadn't happened. Nothing had happened. I climbed out of bed, took her by the arm and guided her out of the room, nudging her along in front of me. I walked her through the kitchen, the serving passage, the living room, into her bedroom, where a man lay asleep. He looked young. Maybe it was one of her pupils, or a new actor from the theatre. When had he come? I left her in bed and went back to my room, still trembling at nearly having spoken.

You're the most theatrical person I've ever met, mum would sometimes say when she was angry with me. So calculatedly mean, she could hiss when her temper got the better of her. It felt like she could hit me. Instead she would shake me, hands gripping my shoulders as if to force some word out of me. I looked into her face, soaked up her despair and anger. I waited for her to stop, waited for her tears to start, the way they always did after an outburst. I braced myself inside, locked myself tight into silence so that no sound would come out. Once, my brother had stepped up behind her and asked: Do you want me to hit her? But mum had merely left the room crying, my brother after her.

If I was afraid of anything, it was that. Physical violence. I knew I couldn't withstand it. That was my weak point, and my brother knew it. It was why he had the power over me. The steady, underlying threat of violence. He could lash out at any time. What would I do then? How was I going to protect what was mine? Mine alone. Dad had hit mum in moments of despair and I'd been petrified, but I don't think mum was. I don't think she was scared. Dad could yell at her, accuse her of sleeping with the whole theatre, of calling the police as soon as he showed his face. I tried to step between them, and would tug on his arm, to make him understand that he had to stop. That he absolutely wasn't to hit her. And that if he did, he would have to hit me too. I knew it was out of the question. He would never have hit me or my brother; he couldn't see us when he was angry, only mum. Preventing dad and my brother from striking out, that was what I was good at. Now there was only my brother to worry about, and he was growing up. Maybe he was growing out of his anger. Maybe

Vendela was a solution. Even if it wouldn't last, I sensed that. But there'd be others like her. Maybe he was growing away from me, so that we'd no longer have to stand in the same room, measuring each other with our eyes.

I hadn't spoken. That was the important thing.

It had been close, but I hadn't spoken.

It would be morning soon. Should I go to bed or stay awake? Perhaps listen to my mum and the man in the kitchen, before she got rid of him? They never stayed for long. Even the thought of someone else at breakfast was inconceivable. She wouldn't have it.

Dad's face there at the dinner table. Completely sunken in on itself. A stagnation and fatigue that seemed enormous. Sitting beside him was like being sucked into darkness, his darkness. He said nothing. He had more than enough with his anxiety disorder. It was a term I heard from mum. Your father suffers from an anxiety disorder, she said. It's a terrible affliction. He can't help things. What had he done? He'd broken in, he'd borrowed money from dubious lenders and bought a farmhouse up north. He was going to keep horses there. Trotting horses. He was going to fish in the river. He was going to catch char. Do what he wanted. But there he was, sitting in our kitchen, ashamed of himself on account of it all. For having ventured to dream that life could go on. That he could make something of himself. The interest payments to the lending company. How was he supposed to manage? He would never move in to that farmhouse. It had been a dream, a dream that now required him to do something, in his other state of mind, under the sway of self-denial and turmoil. The dense darkness of depression. Who was supposed to save him? Mum was. Only she could save him, her sheer primordial force would fix things for him. She could get the loan agreement annulled on the basis of dad not being of sound mind. She could lay into them, make some phone calls, sort things out. Was that what he was hoping? Or was the farmhouse what he wanted, deep down inside himself? It was impossible to tell.

One thing was clear though, and that was that he couldn't cope with anything. That his darkness commanded him to die. He was no use to anyone. A broken man. Mum had chewed him up and spat him out. She'd lived their life as if it were the most natural thing in the world, only then to shut him out. It's the end of the line, she told him. And it was true. It had got to that. But why did she still help him, even when they were divorced? Why was he sitting in our kitchen? Why did she have to sort out his mess, then later be accused of taking everything away from him? Even his farmhouse, he yelled at her when things came to a head for him, when he'd forgotten all about sitting in our kitchen and wishing he was dead. Why did she have to sort everything out for him? Why didn't she let him sink to the bottom like a stone? Why did she have to hold him upright? Because he's your father, she said. Because I loved him once. Because you can't just abandon another person.

Did I ever ask mum to stop seeing him? In as many words? No, I did not. I prayed to God.

I watched her as she sat there in the bedroom with her hot curlers in. She was wearing a denim skirt and a white top she'd knitted herself. She was smoking a cigarette, it lay burning in the ashtray as she wound a strand of hair around a curler. She did her hair every day. Ironed some item of clothing. Rehearsals were starting. It was the first day and the director was coming from Poland. Strand after strand, fastened with a pin until her hair was entirely rolled up against her scalp. She was so beautiful. So shiningly bright and happy. Her joy. Her propensity for joy.

What was I doing home? Was I ill? Why was I looking at her like that? I wanted to be near to her. It was always the same. Was she taking me with her to the theatre? How old was I?

My first day at school. I went with my friend and her family, mum was rehearsing and dad was ill. I felt big, everyone else had their parents with them. I spoke up in a clear voice when my turn came to say my name and when my birthday was. I said yes when the teacher asked if I was looking forward to school. I told her I could already read. I'd decided to excel in every subject. I imagined it would be easy. So much easier than everything else. And it was too. Predictable, with no surprises. It annoyed me now that I'd turned into someone who told lies. What was I trying to prove? Why did I need to make myself better than I was? It was natural that I was the leader. The one who decided who was in and who was out. Only in the tree with my one real friend were things different. The discussions we had there were more equal, and I could never be sure of what would come next.

The scream from the living room tore through the silence of the apartment. The despair of the pupil. She was Medea, betrayed by Jason. She was going to revenge herself. There was no other choice. Mum's voice from inside, calm and objective. Or when suddenly she screamed herself, to demonstrate to her pupil how to release one's despair, so that she might muster the courage and not hold back. Raw despair, that was where she had to go. I took the tube of cod-roe spread and the packet of crisp-bread. Squeezed some globs of the spread onto a piece of the crispbread, put it on a plate and took it with me into my room. I sat down at the desk and listened to the pupil's efforts. It sounded like an effort too, and I knew my mum had already decided the girl lacked talent. The salty spread tasted good with the crispbread. I ate a whole one and had gone back to the kitchen for more when I heard my brother coming in. I decided to stay put in the kitchen. I took another piece of crispbread as if it was nothing, as if being in the kitchen was something I had a right to. I took a glass and filled it with water that rushed from the tap. I sat myself on the counter with my crispbread and spread and waited for him to come in.

He was with someone. It was Vendela. He gave me a look, but Vendela said hello. I stared at her, prompting her to step back, as if to hide behind my brother. As casually as he could, he asked what she wanted to eat. They could toast a couple of sandwiches, he said, how did that sound? Fine, she said. I stayed where I was and watched them while I ate. I watched my brother get the griddle out of the cupboard, then the things for the sandwiches: bread, ham, cheese, tomatoes. It was implicit that I should leave the room whenever he was there, but Vendela being there meant I could stay. As long as she was there, my brother couldn't do a thing. He'd get me back for it, but I didn't think about that. My brother must have explained to Vendela about mum's pupils, because she didn't ask about the screams from the living room. He made an effort to talk to her even though I was still there: They should go to a concert soon, he said. Did she want to sing today, or should they go out instead? I suppose we could have an ice cream in the park, she said.

I thought about what it was like for him, me being there. And for her too. It must have been off-putting, his sister staring like that, without a word. I could have spared him, but for some reason I didn't want to. I didn't want them to feel they had me pinned down, mum and my brother. I didn't want them to think I'd always be in my room.

I heard mum open the door into the hall. In a moment she would say goodbye to her pupil, then come to the kitchen. My brother heard her too, I saw the way he stiffened. Mum's footsteps, so energetic. A second later she was standing there, buoyant. Vendela, how nice to see you again. She glanced at me. I looked back at her and stayed where I was. I needed all my willpower not to disappear back to my room. Well, here we all are, she said, smiling. What plans have you got? We're going out, my brother said, and I couldn't tell if he was angry. He sounded normal. Good idea, it's lovely outside, mum said, and glanced at me again. I couldn't hold out any longer, slid down from the counter and crossed through the kitchen to my room. I closed the door behind me and sank down into the armchair. Then the tears came. They welled in my eyes and trickled down my cheeks.

I cried without a sound, unable to sob, though I was definitely on the verge. I compelled the tears to leave all sound behind them. If I let them flow quickly, it wasn't a problem. I concentrated. Mum started dinner in the kitchen. My brother had gone out with Vendela. What would happen if I went to the kitchen? Would mum tell me her thoughts? I got to my feet, wiped away the tears, which had now subsided, and went to the kitchen again. I sat down at the table. Mum was shaping lamb patties. She turned her head towards me and smiled, but said nothing. She was totally absorbed in what she was doing, and the thought came to me from somewhere that I would have to die.

Dear God who art in Heaven. Look after mum and make her happy. Look after her and let me die.

I lay in bed in the dark and silently uttered my prayer for the first time. Would God hear me straight away, or would he wait? If he waited, how long would I have to wait? Until I was grown up? I'd never looked into the future before, now it was all I could see. I peered ahead in time and saw myself as a teenager like my brother, then as an adult. I took a hard look at myself. This staying silent couldn't possibly last a lifetime.

A full, whole life was unreasonable, I told myself. No one could ask that of me. They'd understand. Deepest down, they surely knew how impossible it was. I'd unleashed my will. Now anything could happen.

The school was on fire. I was walking along the pavement some paces behind my brother with my schoolbag. The smoke could be seen some distance away. The entire top floor was in flames and I was sure it was my fault. That it was my prayer that had brought on the blaze. Later, however, it turned out it had been started by two boys outside the chemistry lab. We all had to go home again. The police cordoned off the area. We couldn't see the firemen as they put the fire out, we weren't allowed in the playground. The smoke rose up. Black clouds, expelled into the sky. It was hard to stop looking at, but eventually my brother tugged at my sleeve and said it was time to go home. We walked next to each other on the pavement and I thought to myself that it was the fire that brought about this sudden closeness. Something external that in some way was a threat to us and led to us now walking together.

I went to my room and sat down in the window. Only the two of us were home, mum was at the theatre. She thought we were at school. The chestnut tree writhed in the wind. How long would the school be closed? I jumped with joy inside at the thought of having to stay home. I put my forehead against the pane, felt the cool glass against my skin and smiled. Maybe we'd get to stay home for a week. Maybe longer. It felt like being off ill, so I got into my pyjamas and went to the kitchen. I found a carton of bilberry soup, then made a cheese sandwich as I listened to my brother's music coming from his room. I sat on the counter and ate, swilling down the sandwich with the fruit soup. I was hungry. I went to the pantry and got some rusks, spread butter on them and dipped them into the soup, sucking on them until they crumbled and dissolved in my mouth. Mum had a first night coming up, so I'd gathered. There was a full dress rehearsal that afternoon in front of an invited audience. She used to ask us not to bring friends home in dress-rehearsal week, having too much on her mind to cope with the place being full. But now she didn't mind anymore. My brother hated the theatre. We'd only been small the time mum had been rolled onto the stage on a slaughter bench wearing only underwear and high-heeled shoes as she sang: *Peckers, gentlemen, please. Behold these ravishing thighs, behold these glorious American tits.* My brother had kept away from the theatre ever since. He hated seeing her made up, hated her wearing high heels. He didn't want her pretending. He was against her work. He was against, and I was in favour. Maybe I would go to the first night after all. Mum used to regale me in the dressing room after a premiere, with sweets and fizzy drinks to celebrate no longer having to rehearse day and night. From then on everything would be more normal, she would have time for us in the afternoons. What was she rehearsing now? Suddenly my heart was thumping. It was the thought of my prayer. That I'd asked to die. Was it really what I wanted? Could I take it back, or was God already getting things ready? At any moment, I could drop dead. Should I pray to God to take it back? Was that possible? I tried to return my mind to the clarity of the day before, when death had seemed like a necessity, like the only possible outcome of my silence. Calmly, I took hold of my thoughts and followed them to the decision. Yes. It was the right thing to do. God would surely let me live a while yet, but a whole life? No, he would spare me adulthood, I was sure of it. I couldn't see myself having any other age than the one I had, the whole idea of growing up felt completely wrong. I wasn't going to let it happen. I couldn't stop time and stay in the present. Growing scared me. My brother resembled a man already, his voice was deep and croaky, his shoulders broader, his nose and jaw more pronounced. He was so tall now. Everything about him had changed, he was no longer the boy in the boat with the fishing net, his eyes watching the fish as they moved in the water. He was something else now. Not quite a grown-up, but then not a child either. There was no going back, it felt so unreasonable.

I avoided mirrors, not wishing to see what growing was doing to me. I was afraid the transformation had already begun.

I knocked on my brother's door. I'm not sure why. I'd not been inside his room for years. Maybe death had frightened me so much that I didn't want to be on my own all of a sudden. My brother's eyes when he came and answered. The way he looked at me, with what seemed like fathomless sorrow and despair. But he opened the door, and I went in. Dark-blue curtains were drawn in front of the window. The light was dim, the desk crammed with computer equipment, a drum machine, the floor packed with amplifiers and loudspeakers, instruments in their stands, fat, worming leads. And the dust, illuminated in the band of light that fell in through the chink in the curtains. I sat down on the unmade bed, straightening the cover before almost flopping down. What was I supposed to do now? What was my intention, going into his room like that, my brother wondered, his eyes telling me so. What do you want here? What are you thinking? How were you supposing we'd get on? I gave a shrug, it was a reflex, something I did a lot, and I found it frightening that it was such a part of me. That it was something I was doing now in my brother's room. Shrugging my shoulders was nearly the same as speaking. I think the shrug was to say: Do what you normally do here. Don't mind me. I think he understood, because he switched the amplifier and the drum machine on. The beat sounded like a fork struck against the kitchen counter. He hung the guitar over his shoulder and plugged in, turned the microphone on. He stepped backwards and looked at me, then began to play, and when a moment later he started to sing it sounded like he was crying. I watched my brother as he stood there singing in English. It was a song about Laura, a girl everyone looked at, but no one ever got to talk to. It felt like I had my brother to myself, as long as he was singing I was allowed to watch him. I stared at his face. He wasn't keeping anything in, was quite unrestrained, singing with all his voice. I was fascinated and hoped the song would never end, but of course it did.

I'd seen him, but now it was finished. He went over to the door and stood there as if to tell me it was time for me to go. I got up and walked out, passing close to him in the doorway. Was I scared? Not then.

I went to my room and sat in the window. What had happened? I'd been to my brother's room. That was all. He'd played a song and I'd watched him. He'd opened himself to me, and why had he done that? Why had he suddenly allowed me to be there, and why had I knocked on his door? The courage of that action made me tremble.

I sat in the window until mum came in through the front door. Then I sat in the armchair with a book and waited for her. I heard her moving about in the kitchen, opening the fridge. I wanted to tell her there'd been a fire at school. I wanted to tell her about the smoke that rose into the sky and about my brother and me having been in his room together. This sudden yearning to speak to her. Where did it come from? I picked up the notebook and a pen. My hand shook as I wrote: *There was a fire at school today.* I went out into the kitchen and placed the notebook on the table. Prodded mum's arm and pointed at it.

She cried. Mum cried. She looked at me with tears running down her face. Her cheeks streaked with mascara. Thank you, she said, and hugged me. I didn't move in her arms. What had I done?

I'd altered something fundamentally. Something whose full scope I couldn't yet see. What did it mean? What would this change bring with it? Did I regret it? I wasn't sure. All I knew was how good it had felt to write down the words. Would I write others? Was the notebook now gradually going to fill up with my thoughts and experiences? What was it that made me feel I had to carry on and write more? Was it just because the words *There was a fire at school today* were now committed to paper and felt like they were carved in stone? There was nothing forcing me. What did mum always say? You're so hard on yourself.

Gingerly, she let go of me, extricated herself from my arms that clung to her. She put her hands on my shoulders and stepped back so as to look me in the eye. This is the start, she said. Everything's going to be all right. Do you understand? I nodded. It was all I could do with her holding me like that, looking straight into me. What was I going to do? What was open and what was closed? Had things swapped places without me noticing, and was I now open to everyone? Could they see straight in? My legs shook and I felt like I was falling. Plummeting to the core of the earth where everything was burning red. The last thing that came to me were the words: You're lost.

You're lost. The words pounded inside me. It felt like someone was hitting me as I sank through the floor. A moment later I was sitting on the back stairs that led from the kitchen, the smell of dust in my nostrils, watching rats as they darted about. I went down the iron staircase, my hand gripping the rail. I met my brother, who passed me slowly without noticing me. At the bottom my mum sat smoking. I went past her, smoothed her blond hair with my hand. I gripped the handle of the door that led out into the courtyard. Cautiously, I pushed it open. The freeways ran in and out, above and below each other. The traffic roared. And there was my dad, bald, the mirror shard pressed to his forehead. Welcome to America, he said, shouting to make himself heard. Welcome to America.

The days that followed the nights after that were ablaze in light, a light so strong I had to close my eyes. I sat in my bed from morning till dusk with my eyes closed. The light cut into me. My dad slithered into my mind and sang, *Wilkommen, Bienvenue, Welcome*, with bells that rang. I tried to get rid of him, but he danced like the blue squiggles behind my eyelids. He alternated between being small and big. Sometimes he turned into a giant, pressing me back against the wall so I could hardly breathe. He sat down on the edge of the bed and blindfolded me. So you never have to see what you all did to me, he said.

Dad disappeared and instead the sea emerged before me. I waded out to the island and watched the herring gulls as they followed the boats. I saw the eagles on the rocks further out. The way they tore at the fish with their beaks and claws. The way they hopped about on the rocks. The rain lashed down and there were geese on the water. I reached up and drew my hand across the sky.

I would never be able to explain why my clothes were wet as I sat and shivered in bed. The puddles that appeared at my feet. I went to the bathroom and peeled off my clothes until I was standing naked in front of the mirror. I was blue from cold. My mouth was stiff and my teeth chattered. I stood for a long time under the shower and felt the warmth come back to me. I dried myself meticulously and crept back to my room where I put on clean, dry clothes.

I was a child. The words that said so came to me as I dried my hair. I didn't need to understand what had happened to me, because there was nothing to understand. Mum was getting the dinner ready in the kitchen. My brother was in his room. Dad was dead. Everything was in its place, even me, so it occurred to me. I was hungry, but I didn't want to go to the kitchen. I thought that if I just stayed where I was, mum would come in with a tray. What had she been doing these past days? Presumably the same as always. But it had passed me by. The blindfold that was on the bed. Did it scare me? The fact that I couldn't explain how it got there. I put it on, and closing my eyes became easier. My eyes relaxed and the darkness surrounded me. Dressed me in black. I listened to the sounds, that sounded like they came from a long way away. The rhythm of the drum machine, and mum moving about. They belonged together, I realised as I sat there on the bed. They were parts of the same music. My throat felt sore. Maybe I was ill. Maybe that was why everything seemed so strange? Dad threatened to come back. He was dead, I told myself, and tried to picture him in front of me, the way he'd been lying there on his own in the flat. I imagined his clothes and the white-green colour of his face. I touched his face and closed his eyes. Again and again, I closed his eyes.

My brother was standing in the room looking at me. He pulled off my blindfold. I hadn't heard him come in. I looked at him.

My heart thumped in my chest and I saw that the intimacy we had experienced was gone again. I couldn't keep him out, he would only force his way in. He dragged me out into the kitchen where mum was sitting at the table, and pressed me down onto a chair before sitting down himself. Mum passed me a dish of grilled chicken drumsticks. Her look told me to eat. We were going to sit together and eat our dinner. I took a drumstick and then some rice and salad. My brother took some too. My mum and brother talked about the rebuilding of the school, how we would soon be starting again, and mum's premiere. Her reviews had been glowing and she was buoyant. I was completely unprepared when my brother suddenly tossed the knife at me. I screamed. The sound that came out of me. My brother and mum smiled and carried on eating. I got up, backed away to my room, where I flung myself onto the bed and wept.

Only the ground floor of the school was in use. Many of our lessons were suspended. The days had gaps in them which I spent in the library. I sat in the same place in the reading room, next to a window looking out on the playground. I read whatever I found. A book about eagles, another on the Greek sagas, another on the flora of the outer archipelagos. None of it stuck, I was drifting on the flow of words, through sentences and pages. Maybe I was only pretending to read so I could sit there in silence. It felt like I was spending those hours there to grow back together again. To feel what had opened now slowly closing. I perceived every sneeze, every footstep, every turn of a page. These were sounds that calmed me. I breathed like someone who'd been underwater for a long time. Heaving in air. I listened to my heart, and made it beat slower and slower.

I was scared. Was I not scared?

The walk home wasn't long enough. The stairs up to the apartment were too few. I was standing in the hall before I even blinked. What had been mine alone was now everyone's. At any time, mum or my brother could appear in my room. I didn't feel safe.

Dear God who art in Heaven. Look after mum. Make her happy and let me die. How many evenings had I asked to die? Surely it had to come soon. Death. I saw no other way.

Mum looked in on me in the evenings when she came home from the theatre. She sat down in the armchair, her eyes rested on me. She always had to tell me how things had gone. How big the audience had been, the scenes that had worked and those that hadn't. She was full of words that found their way inside me. I hadn't touched the notebook since the day of the fire at school, but mum still looked in it every day. I listened to her stories, sensing how every word seeped its way in. I could see it all: the foyer, the lift up to the dressing room, the corridors and the passage that led to the small stage where she was appearing at the time. The play was a comedy, *The Servant of Two Masters.* I could flutter with longing for the theatre. Why couldn't I go with her, the way I used to? I thought about the time a thief had been on the prowl there, how the stage manager had come over the tannoy and advised everyone to lock their dressing rooms. I remember how frightened it made me. The way I made no distinction between a thief and a murderer. At any time, my mum could be murdered. That was what I'd thought. One of the old doormen gave me a piece of chocolate cake to settle me down. It was their *Tempest* project and every actor in the company was involved on stage. Mum had been Mother Earth, her body bombarded by missiles. I was too big now for the theatre. That was the truth. No one would want a kid my age hanging around. Somehow I'd grown without noticing, and now there was no more path. Ahead of me lay only darkness.

I went through my things. The notebook, the filetting knife, the teddy bear I still slept with, my books: *One Thousand and One Nights* and the *Kitty* books, a dictionary. I pressed the blade of the knife against my thumb until the skin split. The blood that appeared soothed me. I went to the bathroom and found a plaster. I saw my face in the mirror. It was me, but it was someone else too. There was something unfamiliar about me, a serenity that ran through my features in a way I hadn't noticed before. I went back through the living room, stood at the window and looked out into the park. The trees were pale green. Summer would soon be here. What would it bring? I tried to steer my mind from the unease that came over me. I definitely didn't want to leave the apartment.

Vendela stopped coming. She'd only been twice, which I supposed was the reason for my brother's bad mood. He didn't nail his door shut, but it was obvious no one was allowed in. I avoided him as best I could. Mostly there was no need for me to see him during the day. Mostly I was allowed to eat in my room. I passed my hand over the radiator and smelled the warm dust.

I'd been such a happy child, mum said. You were always happy. And now you're not. If only you could tell us why. But there's nothing I can say. All I know is that I'm neither happy nor sad. Did I think my thoughts would reach her? She needed comfort as much as anyone else. Her constant worry. Hasn't this gone far enough now? How much longer can you keep it up?

Until I die, I could have said. I could have told her everything.

*

Every day you must make the most of life. Attack the day with purpose, mum told me as I lay in bed. It was what she did. She woke up and directed all her attention first to breakfast, then to herself, the clothes she was going to wear, her face, always done so meticulously and with the kind of objective detachment only she possessed. Everything she did, she did in earnest. My passivity was the worst thing that could happen to her. It got to her where she was most vulnerable. But it wasn't my fault. I hadn't planned or even wanted it that way. It was how I was. I do wish you'd show some purpose, mum said again, with eyes that dwelled.

I climbed out of bed to go to the bathroom. I passed mum on the way and she grabbed hold of me and took me in her arms. We stood there and looked at each other for a moment. She was stronger than me, I had to dig my elbow in for her to let go. Her words, You've got no right to do this, struck me in the back.

I went out to the park, to the leaves unfolding on the trees, to the statues and the café, busy now in the pleasant sun. The warm air smelled faintly of exhaust fumes. What was I doing here among all these dogs and cheerful people? Still, I decided to walk. I passed the dog exercise area, and the library where only grown-ups could come. I followed the path, past the crocus beds, to the café where we used to buy ice cream. Around the hill to the play area, then back to the street with our building in the middle. I crossed over at the crossing, keyed in the code, and went inside to the stairway. I opened the front door and stepped into the apartment. The place was quiet. Mum was washing up after dinner, and my brother was in his room.

I avoided the mirror. The living room seemed huge. Like a great hall, waiting for people. The serving passage with the black-and-white diamond-patterned flooring led me into the kitchen, to mum. She turned around. Looked at me and smiled. Have you been out? How nice.

I helped her put the plates away in the cupboard, the cutlery in the drawer, and wiped the crumbs off the table. After that I went and got the vacuum cleaner and began to do my room. Dust had collected everywhere and the air was stale. I opened the window, then went back out for the cleaning things. I didn't miss a surface. I wanted everything spick and span. I got down on my hands and knees and scrubbed the floor, then ran the cloth over it. By the time I was finished it was gleaming. I got clean sheets from the linen cupboard in the living room. A thud of music came from my brother's room as I went past the door. Mum came out behind me and went through to the hall on her way out to the theatre. Our paths separated and she waved as she left.

When I went back to my room, my dad was there. He was sitting in the armchair whistling. His hair was black and he looked up when I came in. Hello, petal, he said. Nice to see you. He watched me change the bedclothes. You're looking after yourself, he said. That's good. Don't forget, you're the one in charge. I didn't want to look at him, so I sat down with a book and tried to read. You've got to stand up to your mother. Don't give her any slack or she'll take everything. He spoke the way they do in the north, as if his years in the city had never happened. Take no notice of your brother. He'll do you no harm, he added. You've got yourself nicely sorted out. That's the way. I think about the lot of you, you know. I never stop.

I tried to will him away, only I couldn't. His smell filled the room. The aftershave he used. I got up off the bed and went to open the window again. Would a fall from the window do it? Was it high enough? It was you and me together when you were little. We'd be in the park waiting for your mum. Those were the best times. How was I to get rid of him? You used to be with me all the time. I'd bike out to the boat with you. You'd sit there in your little life vest in the prow while I put the nets out. You were always so excited the next morning, when we took them up again. You'd only just learned to talk, but there you'd sit, still as you like, I was never afraid you'd fall in. Just sit there, you would, staring at the fish as they came up out of the water. How could I shut him up? The knife wouldn't help, he was already dead. Your mother doesn't understand, he laughed. She does what she does, that's all. Full steam ahead. I loved her too much. Never love anyone too much. I had to make him stop. I had to get him out of my room. I thought for a moment, then picked up the notebook and wrote: *You're dead. You can't come here.* I put the notebook in his lap and watched him read. So that's what you think, is it? He laughed again. Well, since you ask so nicely.

He was gone.

I lay down on the bed. The room spun, and I was a part of its spinning. Round and round I went, trying to fix my eyes on a point on the ceiling. Only when I put a foot down on the floor did it stop. You're falling away, come back. You're falling away. Twice now I'd written in the notebook. What did it mean?

I went to the kitchen to make some tea.

The coldness my dad had left behind was in everything. I took a mug from the cupboard and heard mum coming in. She stepped into the kitchen and smoothed my cheek. But she said nothing, and I could see that her thoughts were elsewhere. She spread some jam on a couple of rusks, took her plate and went out of the room again. I followed her towards the living room, but stopped at my room and left her to herself.

My room was back to normal. The smell had been aired away and it felt like he'd never been there. Had he been there? I wasn't sure. I read what I'd written in the notebook. Yes, he'd been there. Was he coming back? Should I tell mum?

Once, he came to the school and collected me. My teacher had protested, she told him we were in the middle of something important, but he grabbed my hand and took me with him. We took the bus to Gröna Lund. There was hardly anyone there, we rode the merry-go-round a few times. I had a tummy ache and wanted to go home, but he went on to the next ride and the next one after that. I had candy floss, ice cream, and sweets, and eventually I was sick in a bin. When we left, we took the ferry to Nybroplan and he said why don't we say hello to mum at the theatre. I told him I didn't want to. I wanted to go home. When we got back I went to bed and pretended to be ill. Dad talked to someone on the phone in the kitchen. His voice was so loud. After a while he started crying. I pretended to be asleep when he came into my room in tears. Are you frightened of me? he wept. Are you frightened?

Mum changed. She was no longer as meticulous about breakfast. Often, she slept into the mornings with her new boyfriend. He was a young and promising director at the theatre and it was his play she was in now. My brother and I would be left to ourselves. I sprinkled the bilberries on the yoghurt the way mum did and put the bread and cold cuts out. My brother let himself be waited on. Occasionally, he ruffled my hair with his big hands.

Mum laughed a lot. She laughed at everything my brother said and when talking with friends on the phone. She was happy, and I told myself it was good that she was absorbed in something other than me. My brother said nothing, but I knew he didn't care for having a stranger in the apartment. As for me, I avoided him as best I could. His blond curls and wide mouth at the table. His name was Ulrik and he was from Denmark. Sometimes I thought he hardly looked older than my brother.

I supposed everything was all right. There was no more talk of the specialist, mum's thoughts were elsewhere. She and Ulrik would sit entwined on a chair, or they chased each other around the apartment, mum shrieking with laughter. I liked that she was so happy, and sometimes I'd pray to God for Ulrik to stay. His youth was against him in that respect, I think mum knew that, but she didn't seem to worry about it. I think she just wanted to be happy in the moment. Ulrik liked to cook. There was always something simmering away on the cooker, and they would eat together after the play. Ulrik stayed in with us in the evenings and got dinner ready, set the table nicely in the living room, aerated the wine.

Everything had to be ready for when mum came home. I heard the way they laughed together as they ate. It struck me how much like kids they were. It was as if we'd swapped places without noticing. As if me and my brother were the grown-ups.

Occasionally, dad would turn up and watch me as I sat in my room, but it didn't bother me and usually he went away again as quietly as he'd come. One time, he said so much had gone wrong since he died. That mum couldn't be trusted. Never trust a woman, he said. As if he knew I'd never become one.

But I didn't think about death that much. It was as if my thoughts wanted to be elsewhere. I longed to be in the light from the sea, to be sitting in the prow of the boat, before everything had gone wrong. Before illness came and smothered our lives together. I wanted to be stepping out onto the islets with my brother, mum, and dad. My brother and I looking for birds' eggs. I think there was another child with us, a girl who lived on our street. Sofia with the long hair, who wanted me to be her baby sister. She put me in a pram once and took me for a walk. I remember the faces leaning in to look at me. The way they recoiled at the big baby who lay there. Then the nervous chuckles. Oh, so it's a game you're playing. Sometimes, when dad went too far with the bottle and became threatening, we'd retreat to Sofia's house. But he always came after us. He smashed a window there and climbed in. Stood in the living room complaining to Sofia's parents about mum, while I held my hands over Sofia's ears, thinking it wouldn't be good for her to hear the things he was saying. It was always something about some man mum had been playing around with, and I knew it wasn't the sort of thing to be broadcast. The ambulance that pulled up slowly outside, and me trying not to draw his attention to it, so he wouldn't run away. I'd dreamt about them coming to get him. Men in white coats who took him away and locked him up for good.

Did I say that I didn't think about illness? That's not entirely true. It was as if every thought ended there. It's not easy growing up.

I tidied my room, cleaned the window with a cloth and the squeegee, dusted the bookshelf, vacuumed and washed the floor. Over and over, with the cloth and the scrubbing brush. I dried the wet floor and binned the clothes that had got too small for me. It soothed me to get the place cleaned, the smell of chemicals mingling with the air from the courtyard. I kept the window open, even when I slept. Mum bought me new floorcloths, I would never use the same one twice. It felt like my body sang when I was cleaning, as if it had been longing for something to do, as if it had tired of my sitting down and needed a change. Mum had started listening to music. Now her music came together with my brother's, and the apartment resonated. It was as if she were shedding all responsibility, as if she had been relieved of some heavy weight. She sparkled, sparkled so brightly. I'd never seen her so happy. She and Ulrik couldn't get enough of each other. Her joy infused us. The atmosphere at home had always been dependent on her. The way she dealt with dad. Her feeling safe was the important thing, and now she felt safe. Nothing bad could happen to her anymore. I ate the food they made together. I saw the way they lit up the apartment and felt this new contentment would last forever. That was why the note from my teacher was so poorly timed. The headmaster wanted to see us, to discuss my situation at school. There was a date and a time. The appointment was already arranged, no ifs or buts. Mum spoke to me. If only I knew what you wanted, she said. Deep down. She accentuated the words, deep down, like the actress she was, and I thought to myself that she wasn't being sincere. That she knew what I wanted, that everyone knew, if only they had the courage to answer the question themselves. Before the meeting she brushed my hair and curled it with the curlers. She ironed my clothes and dressed me. A dazzling white blouse and dark-blue jeans. Then, meticulously, she put her face on and changed into a dress. We smelled so fresh and clean as we walked along the pavement together. Now it was us against them. We needed to stand up for ourselves.

The headmaster shook mum's hand, glancing briefly at me, making some polite remarks, asking her how things were at the theatre, as people often did. Mum answered vaguely, and he invited us to take a seat. He was a bald man with glasses. I'd never seen his office before. He looked like he belonged in another age and smoothed his brow repeatedly with the tip of a finger, as if it were an important preliminary to the matter at hand.

We've rather a situation, he said. Ellen won't speak, we realise that. But Britta, her class teacher, is unsure as to how to proceed. Since Ellen won't write either, we don't know how she's getting on. It's becoming increasingly hard to see how we can have Ellen progress to Year 7. That said, we've no reason to believe there's anything at all wrong with the child's intelligence. But we do have a difficult situation on our hands, and I would very much like to hear your own thoughts on the issue. At this point he paused and looked at us in turn, and all I wanted was to back out of the room and run, but I couldn't, I was stuck there. I knew mum felt the same way. That all she wanted was to get up and leave and take me with her, to run to the convenience store and buy ice cream and celebrate that we'd got away with it. Instead we sat there, soaking it up.

I should like to alleviate your concerns. Mum's voice sounded deep as she spoke. Ellen—, she went on. I didn't care to hear my name, it had been a long time since anyone had used it. Ellen has begun to communicate at home, using a notebook. I see her moving in the right direction. I think the best thing would be to wait and see before doing anything drastic.

Have you sought medical advice?

I hated him. I wanted to beat him to a pulp.

As yet, no. I'm sure it's going to pass of its own accord. There's nothing wrong with her.

The headmaster scrutinised me. I felt forced to meet his gaze and stared into the piggy eyes that peered out through his glasses.

What do you say, Ellen? Just nod or shake your head. Do you want to move up with the rest of your class to Year 7 next term? I carried on staring at him. He had to understand I was stronger than him.

I don't think there's much point to this, I heard mum suddenly say. Ellen's not going to communicate with you. You're wasting our time, and if I didn't know better I'd think the only reason you called us in here was to satisfy your own personal curiosity. You know perfectly well she's not going to speak to you in any way. I suggest we conclude this meeting immediately and that no further steps be taken. Mum stood up. I could hear how angry she was. I followed suit and we turned and left. No one tried to stop us. We strode along the corridor, down the stairs and out through the gates. The air was mild and pleasant, birds could be heard above the traffic. I was proud of what mum had done, she wouldn't be pushed around by anyone, least of all a school headmaster. Nevertheless, I cried. Mum wiped my tears and said: Don't ever be anything other than the way you are. She was scared, I could tell that. I imagined how the doctors and the social services would come to our fine and spacious apartment and look for things that were wrong. Mum would show them a splendid, perfectly kept home. There was nothing wrong with us, she would say, and they would have to agree. Everyone would see that we were a family of light. We were untouchable, because that was how mum wanted it.

That evening, mum tucked me in the way she used to when I was little. Perhaps I still was little, I wasn't sure. It was hard to place the person I'd become on a timescale. Maybe I was already grown up? Maybe growing had got me a long time ago? She gave me tea to drink and two delicate sandwiches with little rolls of cheese and ham, and cucumber with the edges cut off, and they were delicious. She stroked my arm absently while I ate. I knew it was to calm her down. She watched me from the armchair as I fell asleep.

Ulrik. When did he go? It was like I'd forgotten him even before he left. Mum seemed to forget him too, I couldn't see that she was unhappy, or that she missed him. An old, familiar mood settled over the apartment.

My brother nailed his door shut again. Dad kept away, or else it was me who made sure. It was a delightful time. We looked after ourselves, there was nothing to disturb us, and the fact that summer would soon be upon us didn't seem as alarming anymore. We were staying at home in the apartment. Anything else was unthinkable. I asked myself how life was meant to be lived, but found no answer. Nothing came to me when I tried to unravel the thread.

My room was hot. The sun beat against the pane. I sat in the window with my eyes shut. Blue squiggles darted behind my eyelids. Sometimes I fell asleep like that, and in sleep I was talking like everyone else. Effortlessly and without thinking about it. I would be rowing a boat with my friend, around and around the lake. Or we'd come running from the house, squealing with joy, pulling off our clothes on the jetty before diving in. Swimming underwater, our hair wafting. Far beneath the surface, to the big rock we tried to budge.

I'd be woken by an arm flopping from my side, or a sudden nod of my head. Who was

I in sleep? It was as if a different time took over, with more room in it for life, a time that posed no questions to my existence. There, in dreams, I simply lived, as if it were the simplest thing in the world. Nothing to ponder or worry about. I imagined that was what it was like for most people, perhaps even my mum and brother too. Maybe it was my worrying that was stopping me from growing, stopping the force that was meant to proceed on its own.

I took my mattress and cover with me onto the balcony. Were there thoughts in my head? Perhaps that my dad would not be shinning up the drainpipe again. That I felt safer now than ever before. I got my bed ready and sat down for a moment in the wicker chair with my feet up on the rail. I took one of mum's cigarettes from the packet on the little table and lit it. The smoke made me cough, but I persevered and looked at the stars. It was after midnight. Mum was already asleep in her bed. I sucked the smoke gingerly into my lungs and wondered if it was something I could start to do. The warm air that drifted in over the balcony was slightly damp, with a suggestion of exhaust fumes. I switched the torch on that was lying on the table and shone the light into the darkness. A bird flapped out of a tree. I pointed the beam at the refuse room and the clothes lines, moving it from one thing to another.

So this is where you're hiding. Mum's voice woke me up. I was under the cover on the balcony. I've been looking for you everywhere. Your brother's gone to school. I pulled the cover up over my head again, wanting to remain where I was, nice and warm. Mum went away again; I stayed put. When she came back she was carrying a tray with breakfast on it. Two glasses of freshly squeezed orange juice, two bowls of yoghurt and bilberries, bread topped with cheese and cress. She arranged everything on the table and sat down with the newspaper. We'll have an easy day, she said. I sat down in the other chair and started to eat. Do you want coffee too? she said. Now that you've started smoking. It was like she could see everything, perhaps even my thoughts, so I tried to think of nothing in particular. The breakfast was lovely. I decided to spend the day on the balcony and felt joyful at the prospect. The coffee tasted bitter, though mum had put lots of milk in. I drank it in small sips and imagined the changing colours of the hours as they passed before my eyes. The morning was yellow, the afternoon green, the evening a purple blush. Mum looked content, she was reading an article and concentrating. Her pupils weren't due until after lunch. She had all the time in the world. No rehearsals, only the play in the evenings. A play she'd been in for a long time, that didn't demand much of her. She wasn't nervous when she woke up in the mornings.

She lit a cigarette and offered me one. I took it and allowed her to light it for me, unsure what she was thinking. We smoked in silence. Each in our own world. Perhaps she was thinking about Ulrik now being back in Copenhagen, or perhaps she wasn't thinking at all. I pictured my classmates sitting in the classroom having geography. I'd already got better at sucking the smoke into my lungs.

I fetched some comics from inside, put them down on the table and picked up the one on top. It was an old issue of *Penny*. I lay on the mattress with the cover on top of me and read about a fire in a stable. Every now and then, I lit a cigarette. Mum had left the packet on the table. I read one comic after another. After *Penny* I turned to *The Phantom*, then to *Agent X9*. The sun shone warmly on me, the hours went pleasantly by. A breeze tugged occasionally at the pages, flapping the paper gently as I read. Mum was in the kitchen with the radio on. She'd opened the window onto the balcony so I could hear too. It was classical, and framed my comic world and cigarettes perfectly. It occurred to me that I might be happy.

I helped mum with lunch in the kitchen, poured the egg yolks carefully into the carbonara and grated the Parmesan. We took linen napkins with us onto the balcony and sat down with our plates in our laps. Mum had turned the music up. It surrounded us completely. It felt like we were celebrating something without knowing what. Perhaps it was just the moment, perhaps it was something more. I ate everything up, and then mum decided we should have ice cream and chocolate sauce. I went to the kitchen and measured out one part sugar, one part chocolate powder, and one part water, stirring it all together in the pan until it thickened and I poured it over the ice cream in the two bowls. I devoured it and went for seconds, thirds, fourths, until I was so full I had to lie down on the mattress again. The sky was bright blue and I lay looking up at mum, who sat with her feet up on the rail the way I'd done the evening before when I'd sat smoking. The doorbell rang, a sonorous vibration in the kitchen, and she stubbed her cigarette, got to her feet, and went out to receive her first pupil of the day.

I returned to my comics. My thoughts followed the frames, exploring every pen stroke. The curtain flapped in the breeze and the music was still on loud. I lay back and closed my eyes, the songs of small birds filled my ears and before long I slept, their voices inside my head.

When I woke up, my brother was on the balcony too. He sat there looking at me.

What did he want? He never came out there.

He went inside again and I wondered how long he'd been sitting there. I heard him nail the door shut and sat down in the wicker chair and looked over the wall into the next yard. A cold wind had come with him and the leaves rustled in the trees. I went back inside, dragging the mattress with me into my room, sensing that my brother wasn't going to allow me to sleep one more night on the balcony. I thought about who actually decided things in our house and ended up realising that we all probably thought it was someone else. Maybe my brother thought it was me who decided, just as I thought it was him and mum thought it was her, even if she actually knew it wasn't. It was as if the calm that sometimes descended on us was dependent on such a fine-grained network of understanding and good will that no one felt inclined to break with the implicit order of things. Everyone needed to contribute, otherwise it fell apart. The network felt strong and extremely vulnerable at the same time. My brother could pull things down whenever he liked. He knew that. Mum could decide to stop doing all the things she did to keep us together. And me? What could I do? I had stretched the system to breaking point with my refusal to speak, exerting a prolonged and steady strain on the structure, which had yielded accordingly to accommodate my silence. I had rearranged the furniture, and it was as if our home were still trying to get its breath back after all the upheaval. But soon we would settle. So far, we had come through this displacement of all things. We were still under pressure, from the school, from the headmaster and the specialists, but mum steered confidently around them now, as if she knew inside that they weren't going to make things better. And then there was God. God, who was going to cut my life short. I could not imagine my mum and brother at the funeral, could not dwell on such fantasies. They scared me. The thought of my mum and brother without me was horrible. The two of them on their own. Had I consciously or unconsciously forgotten to pray to God these last evenings before bed?

One thing I did know was that we were still in a kind of ecstasy after dad had died. How could we have been so fortunate? It felt like we'd been living under the foot of a giant pressing us down and now suddenly the giant was gone. Maybe that was why I'd been so fond of being at the theatre. Dad had no sway there. At the theatre, art was in charge, and the people there would have done everything in their power to prevent him wrecking a performance. Not even dad could get onto the main stage and snatch my mum away. She was safe there, and I, sitting in the auditorium, was inside that safety zone too, that sense of total security that lasted a couple of hours and which appeared so magical and sparkling to me. Maybe that was why I no longer felt the same need for the theatre. Because dad was dead and nothing else felt quite as threatening to us. And yet something told me we were now beginning to drift apart, whereas previously we'd stood together. It disturbed me that this could be happening. I suppose I'd imagined a blissful existence in which all three of us sat watching films in mum's big bed, the way we did after we were set free. We appeared at her bedside as if arriving for a party, with sweets and video cassettes we watched on the brand new video machine. That was the thing about growing up. Certain things belong to certain times. The thought of my brother and I in the same bed seemed inconceivable now. Did I miss it? Was I trying to relive my childhood, only this time without dad? Looking at the photos I could see myself as a baby, in a white sleeping suit, dad smiling as he lifted me up above the bed. I could see myself as a four-year-old standing next to a pike dad had caught, so everyone could see how little I was and how big the pike was. Happy snaps from a happy childhood. Mum's smile at the flash bulb. You could sense the life force inside her vibrating in that small moment of immortalisation. A mother and father. Two young children. All the nights that turned into mornings. The festive occasions, visitors and friends. Mum and dad. Me and my brother. And then suddenly the day when dad collapsed at the table. The way he slumped in his chair, then took to his bed in the cabin and refused to get up. Mum had to deal with the nets. That was the first time. Nothing could make him get up, he lay there all summer. Mum packed the picnic basket even more meticulously than before, and we bathed on the island from morning till evening. We were a family of light. The meatballs tasted wonderful in the sun, and I gazed and gazed out over the glittering sea. Was that when we first realised we were better off without him?

After that came the degradation. I didn't know the word for it then, but I felt it with every part of my body. Like the night I wasn't allowed to go to the toilet, because I had to sit on the chair and listen to my dad sing that song he liked, all of a sudden it was so vitally important to him. As if somehow the song explained his whole being. His entire situation. I remember what it felt like to eventually wet myself, the feeling of it seeping through my pants and nightdress, running out over the chair and onto the floor. I remember crying, and dad, who carried on singing until morning, when eventually he went to bed without a word.

Usually, my thoughts would stop at that moment in the boat. Perhaps I hoped it would last forever then. My dad's smile as my brother pulled in another fish. So meticulous he was, my brother. The way he followed the fish as they swam and scooped them up without disturbing the net. Mum, dressed correctly on every occasion. Maybe she was always in a play? Functional outdoor wear, hair in a perfect ponytail, her smile that seemed always to be directed towards some invisible camera. The family together, an outing. Perhaps the dead turbot floating at the surface was the first sign that something was wrong. My brother, thinking it to be alive, hauled it gleefully into the boat. That stinking fish, which the sea birds had already pecked. For a moment, we didn't know what to do with it. My brother's indignation and embarrassment when he realised. He felt stupid for having been so excited and directing dad to where the fish lay in the water. He'd shown himself up. We looked at him. We looked at each other. What were we going to do? What were we supposed to do with each other?

Dad, who eventually dropped the fish back over the side, and mum, who didn't know what face to wear. For a second, we looked at each other with fear in our eyes. What was happening? Subdued, we headed out towards another island, our brief exchanges lacking the ease mum normally ensured. She didn't know how to act. She unpacked the cooler bag. Poured some squash for my brother and me. Coffee for dad and herself. We were a family of light. A family of light.

On the Design

As book design is an integral part of the reading experience, we would like to acknowledge the work of those who shaped the form in which the story is housed.

Tessa van der Waals (Netherlands) is responsible for the cover design, cover typography, and art direction of all World Editions books. She works in the internationally renowned tradition of Dutch Design. Her bright and powerful visual aesthetic maintains a harmony between image and typography and captures the unique atmosphere of each book. She works closely with internationally celebrated photographers, artists, and letter designers. Her work has frequently been awarded prizes for Best Dutch Book Design.

The photograph on the cover is by Dana Menussi, an interior designer and photographer living in Brooklyn, NY. The image was taken in Phoenix, Arizona, and the girl in the shot is Menussi's niece. The photographer says, 'We were hanging out at my in-laws' pool and I was struck by the strength of her expression. Veronica's beauty and maturity had always captured me, and I often took pictures of her as she was growing up.'

The cover has been edited by lithographer Bert van der Horst of BFC Graphics (Netherlands).

Suzan Beijer (Netherlands) is responsible for the typography and careful interior book design of all World Editions titles.

The text on the inside covers and the press quotes are set in Circular, designed by Laurenz Brunner (Switzerland) and published by Swiss type foundry Lineto.

All World Editions books are set in the typeface Dolly, specifically designed for book typography. Dolly creates a warm page image perfect for an enjoyable reading experience. This typeface is designed by Underware, a European collective formed by Bas Jacobs (Netherlands), Akiem Helmling (Germany), and Sami Kortemäki (Finland). Underware are also the creators of the World Editions logo, which meets the design requirement that 'a strong shape can always be drawn with a toe in the sand.'